The Door to the Past

Michael Banister

Ravenous Press
Berkeley, California

Published by Ravenous Press

Printed in the United States of America.

First Edition: October 2025

10 9 8 7 6 5 4 3 2 1

ISBN 978-1-950562-71-8

Cover and book design by Andrew Benzie

Dedicated to animal welfare organizations worldwide.

CHAPTER ONE

Felix finally made up his mind. In couple of minutes, after Mike and Nora leave the back door open and start making their breakfast, Felix would escape! He was a large Maine Coon cat that Mike and Nora had adopted from a shelter specializing Maine Coons. He liked living with Mike and Nora, but was getting a little bored. He had never been out of the back yard. There was one place in the backyard where it seemed possible to jump over the fence and escape through Carol and Ken's yard and out to the street.

"Easier than I thought," Felix said after he jumped down in the middle of Carol's vegetable garden. He didn't waste any time hanging around—he didn't want to run into Ken's dog, a tall, nosy greyhound named "Kab." Felix often heard Ken tell friends that he got the greyhound from his cousin in Oklahoma. His cousin had a pen full of greyhounds that he rented out to farmers who used them to chase down and kill the coyotes that were killing the sheep and calves.

Felix made a dash along the far side of Carol's house, across the street, and up the street to Jan the piano tuner's house.

There was a creek next to Jan's house that had crossed under the street and come out in the open where her driveway began. It went on for a hundred feet or so before being covered over again after it ran alongside Jan's house. But just where the creek emerged at the beginning of Jan's driveway, the ground sloped down to the creek bed, which was almost dry now that it was summer.

Felix had heard stories about the creek—mostly from his roommate, Abigail, who claimed to have explored it more than once. Abigail was a large Maine Coon like Felix. So were their friends Freddie and Fiocco, who lived with Erica and Lorenzo on the other side of Mike and Nora's house. Felix had heard Lorenzo tell Mike that he and Erica decided to adopt Maine Coons after they got to know Felix and Abigail.

Freddie and Fiocco liked to brag about how they had travelled the creek all the way under Kansas Street from Jan's house to Tony's house across the street, and beyond to where it ran uncovered alongside a field. That was where Felix intended to go today.

Feeling his way carefully, Felix climbed down the steep bank to the creek bed. Looking to his right, past Jan's house, he saw the entrance to another culvert that led somewhere dark and unfriendly looking. The culvert was much narrower than the culvert leading to Tony's house.

Felix started walking into the one to the left. It was short, and he could see the daylight coming from the other end. In less than a minute he emerged, just on the inside of Tony's front fence.

"Wow! I've always wanted to see what Tony's yard looked like." As he walked carefully along the creek bed, Felix looked up at Tony's yard. Besides the main house there was a small cottage that looked like it was going to fall down any minute. Next to that were two huge doghouses. When Felix saw the doghouses, he worried that Tony's two dogs might be sleeping. Tony like to brag to his friends that one of the dogs was Rolph, a Rhodesian Ridgeback that he had bought from a friend who brought the dog home with him from Africa. According to Tony's friend, he used Rolph to chase down and kill hyenas, and sometimes even chased away lions that were menacing farmers' flocks. Tony said that his other dog was actually a full-blooded wolf, a HUGE wolf that he had adopted from an animal sanctuary, raised as a puppy, and named Lukan. Felix didn't want to wake either one. They were even nosier than Kab, and Felix was a little scared of them. Felix wanted to get past the houses and to the field ASAP.

Up ahead he saw eucalyptus trees on both sides of the creek, a field beyond the trees on the right and a gravel road that dead-ended at the trees on the left. Pausing for a couple of minutes to take in the view directly ahead of him as the creek continued on its way, Felix turned to his right and started climbing up the steep bank, trying not to slip on what seemed like hundreds of eucalyptus acorns. When he got to the top he turned around and gazed across the creek at the gravel road disappearing in the distance. "I'm pretty sure that road runs along the backyards of the houses behind my house." He kept that thought in his mind just in case he decided not to return home via the creek.

He turned back around and looked at the field beyond the eucalyptus trees next to him on the right bank. The field was a square about 100 yards on a side with houses on the left and right and a busy street straight ahead. The field was mostly clumps of grass and a few tall bushes. In the middle stood a falling-down shack of some kind. "I'm gonna check that out. I'll bet Abigail has never seen it; maybe Fiocco has—she's been everywhere."

Felix decided he would head straight for the shack, dashing to each clump of bushes along the way to stay out of sight. The first bush was about 20 feet ahead, slightly to the right. He no sooner got to the bush than he saw a large hawk swoop down in front of him and snatch up a rat as it was running from the bush. "Damn! The rat must have been running from me! Poor little devil." Felix, despite his size, had never been much of a hunter.

Figuring the hawk was too busy eating the rat to think about preying on a cat, especially a huge Maine Coon, Felix made two more dashes to the bushes between him and the shack. "Piece of cake," he said as he caught his breath under a huge ceanothus bush that was almost a tree. The shack was now about 20 feet ahead of him. He could see a large entrance with the door hanging ajar. "Probably was some kind of garage, or maybe a barn." He wondered if there had been a house next to it in the past.

One more mad dash and Felix made it to the shack. He stepped carefully inside and took a look around. "Not much to see. Looks like a bunch of junk."

Just then he heard a sound he hadn't heard since he lived with a bunch of other foster kittens. "It's a cat, a young one!" Following the sound, he walked through the boxes, bales of hay, a tall cabinet and gardening tools. Between two stacks of boxes, he saw a terrible sight—a dead, emaciated adult cat. Felix followed the sound of the kitten and found her hiding between two hay bales "Ah, so there you are, little one. Is that your mom over there?"

The kitten stared at Felix for a moment before she answered. "Yes. She's dead. Her milk dried up, and she couldn't catch any more mice or rats. Hawk got them before she could; the hawk almost got me like it did my sister. One of my brothers ran off, and a snake got the other one. Where'd you come from?"

Felix saw that she was a young Maine Coon like him. He walked up to her and licked her on the top of her head. "I was just exploring the neighborhood and decided to check out this field." Felix sat down and groomed her some more. As the young cat purred, Felix looked back at the way he came and made up his mind. "Say, why don't you come home with me? I think I could talk my people into taking you in. My roommate Abby would love to have another cat to play with. What do you say?"

The kitten looked up at Felix and said, "Sure; I'd love to come with you!"

Felix led the young cat back to the creek, taking care to duck into bushes along the way to avoid being targeted by the hawk. "Decision time," he said aloud as he looked at the gravel road and then to his left where the creek led back through Tony's yard, with its dog, and beyond that the culvert. "Okay, we're going along the creek; the road looks a little scary."

Felix helped the little cat climb down the bank. "You ever gone down to the creek?"

"No way; my mom told us all to stay put while she did all the hunting and exploring."

Once down, Felix said, "Okay, the rest is pretty easy. Except we may have to run when we get to Tony's yard up there."

"Why run?"

"Tony's got two dogs, and I don't want to wake them up. Just follow me and do what I do."

They were in luck—the dogs were asleep, and there was nothing scary inside the culvert under the street. When they climbed up the bank at Jan's house, Felix said to the little cat, "From here on, you gotta remember how to get here. I have a feeling you'll come here again and again."

From there, it was an easy jog back to Carol's back yard. At the fence, Felix said, "We're almost home. Over this fence, and then we'll see how Abby reacts. I think she's gonna like you. Listen, when she comes over to sniff you over, you just let her, and rub yourself all over her. She used to be a momma, and you're still young, so it'll be easy to get on her good side. And if Mike or Nora sees you with Abby and me, I think they'll do the right thing."

As it turned out, Felix called it right. The little cat had a home.

CHAPTER TWO

The little Maine Coon called herself Guava. She was relieved to be safe. But at the same time seemed anxious about something. Felix and Abby noticed this, and Abby asked, "What's the matter? You still upset about your brother, the one who ran off?"

"Yes, I'm worried about him. He was living in the barn, too. Until last month, the night of the full moon. He went into the old tool cupboard again, and I'm worried he can't come back out."

Abby said, "What do you mean, he went into the tool cupboard? Why would he do that?"

Felix said, "Are you talking about that dirty old cupboard? Why would he go inside that?"

"Yeah, that's it. He's gone into it twice before, said it's bigger on the inside than it looks on the outside. He said the cupboard has a back door. But he only stayed overnight. He always came back out before dawn. This time, he didn't come back out. I tried to open the door but couldn't get it open."

Abby said, "Whoa! You're not making any sense. What's in the tool cupboard that a cat would want to go inside, let alone stay all night?"

"Mango—that's his name—said the back door of the cupboard is a doorway to another place or another time, something like that. He told me he would always come back out, but this time he didn't."

At this point, Guava started crying. She said, "Look, tonight's another full moon. You gotta help me get the door open. Maybe Mango will come back through."

Abby said, "What's the matter with the door?"

"I don't know. It's stuck almost closed. I couldn't pull it open like before. You gotta help me."

Abby said to Felix, "Let's get over there and see if we can pull it open."

Felix said, "I think we'll need some muscle. Let's see if we can get Tony's dogs to help us. Maybe we could all pull on the rope that's tied to the cupboard door and pull the door open."

Abby said, "And don't forget Carol and Ken's dog Kab. Kab's pretty strong. He'd probably love to try. Tony's two dogs are Rolph and Lukan. They're huge and very strong. Lukan is actually a wolf. They're pretty bored sitting around Tony's yard all day, nothing to do."

Guava said, "Are you sure they would help us? Do they know you and Felix?"

Abby said, "Well, they've met Kab a couple of times, I think. I heard Ken tell someone that Kab is a Greyhound and that his previous owners in Oklahoma used to send him out into the farm to chase down and kill coyotes! He's huge and fast."

Guava said, "Hey, I just remembered that Mango said the full moon's the time to go through the second door, the one that goes to another world. Do you think Kab and Tony's dogs would be able to join us tonight?"

Felix said, "Like Abby said, the dogs are pretty bored most of the time. And night time would be perfect—their people go to bed early."

CHAPTER THREE

First stop—Kab's house. Guava, Abby and Felix stood next to Carol's fence and tried to decide whether to hop the fence or just call out to Kab. Abby said, "Let's not jump over just yet. I'll just call out loudly and see if he hears me." She let out a screech like when she used to get into arguments with other cats. She waited a minute and tried again. Nothing.

Felix said, "Let me try something." He jumped to the top of the fence and whispered loudly, "Ka-a-a-a-a-b! Are you awake?"

That did it. Kab came staggering around the corner of Carol's house blinking his eyes and staring into the dark night. "Whaaat? Who is it? Is that you Felix?"

"Yeah, it's me. And Abby and our new friend. We need your help."

"My help? Doing what? Whoever heard of a dog helping a cat!" He paused and then said, "I recognize Abby, but who's that other cat with you?"

"That's Guava. I rescued her from that abandoned shack up in the field."

Abby said, "Kab, let me remind you that you HAVE helped a cat before. You helped me when you chased that coyote out of your yard, remember? Here's what we want you to do for us. Do you know that old shack in the field across the creek from Tony's house? Well, Felix rescued Guava here from the shack. Her mom's dead body is inside and her brother got stuck in the tool shed that's inside the shack. We need some muscle to open the stuck door of the tool shed. Think you can do it?"

Kab puffed up his chest and wagged his tail. "Sure, I can do it! Hey, I've got an idea. Let's get Tony's two dogs to join us. Those dogs are super dogs! And they know me. Plus, Carol and Ken are visiting friends in Berkeley. They didn't say when they would be back."

Abby and the other two cats watched as Kab backed up and then ran full speed at Carol's fence. Then he jumped over it! He landed in Mike and Nora's yard and ran up to Abby, Guava and Felix, wagging his tail. "How about that! First time for me, but it won't be the last!"

The four of them didn't waste any time hanging around in Mike and Nora's yard. They went out the open gate on the side of the house, turned left and trotted down the street to Tony's house. Then Abby said, "As you can see, Tony's yard is completely enclosed by a high wall. To get into his yard, we'll have to cross the street here to the front of Jan's house. There's a creek that runs under the street connecting Jan's and Tony's houses. The creek is open, so we can go down to it at Jan's front yard and follow it under the street to Tony's yard."

Kab looked nervous. "What do you mean, go under the street? That sounds creepy."

Felix shook his head and said, "Not creepy at all. There's a tunnel under the street. We just walk through the tunnel from Jan's yard to Tony's yard. The only tricky part is not to be surprised by the dogs." He paused and then said, "Kab, that's where you come in. You said you know the dogs. Have you ever actually met them?"

Kab nodded. "Yeah, a couple of times. Tony walks them up and down the sidewalk every day, sometimes a couple of times a day. And he stops to talk to Carol or Ken if they're in the front yard. I was in the yard with Ken just coming back from a walk when Tony walked up with his dogs and started talking to Ken. The dogs looked at me, wagged their tails and wanted to come closer. But Tony kept them back."

Abby said, "Their names are Rolph and Lukan."

"Yeah, I heard Tony call them that. He told Mike that Rolph, the larger dog, was a Rhodesian Ridgeback, and Lukan was a full-blooded wolf. Do you think they'd be willing to help us get through the tool cupboard?"

Felix said, "Yeah, I do. I think they must be very bored sitting around in Tony's yard all the time. The only time they get to go anywhere is when Tony takes them up the block and back. Not even around the block! So, what do you say? I say let's go now. Tony goes to bed early and the dogs will be restless with nothing to do. Let's give them something to do!"

CHAPTER FOUR

It didn't take the four of them very long at all to get to Jan's yard and climb down to the creek. They stood looking into the dark tunnel. Kab said, "Sure looks creepy! And dark! How short is it?"

Felix said, "It's only as long as the street is wide. Not long at all. You can sort of see the light on Tony's garage on the other side of the tunnel. It's just a glimmer. Let's start walking. Follow me; I did this before when I rescued Guava."

The tunnel was short, but muddy, smelly and creepy. Kab kept whining until they got to the other end. Then he started wagging his tail when they emerged and could see Tony's yard up to the left. They were still in the creek, with the field and abandoned shack beyond the right bank. Guava said, "Oh, there's that creepy place! That's where my mom died and my brother Mango disappeared."

Felix said, "Okay, Kab. It's your time to shine, brother! Climb up the bank and see if you can see Rolph and Lukan. We'll wait down here until you talk to them. Tell them our plan and that your three cat friends are waiting down here in the creek."

Kab looked forward to meeting Rolph and Lukan again. He was sure they would recognize him and be interested in getting out of the yard for a while, taking a vacation, so to speak. Plus, doing a good deed. Carefully, slowly and quietly, Kab climbed up the left embankment and crept into Tony's yard. Expecting that the dogs would be asleep, he was pleasantly surprised to see both of them standing a few feet away wagging their tales and looking at him.

Kab walked up to them wagging his tail. They took a few steps toward him and began sniffing him all over. Then they touched noses. Kab decided he would complement them and said, "You guys are huge!" Looking around at Tony's yard he said, "What a great place to live! Right on the creek!"

Rolph, the Ridgeback, said, "Yeah, well, it may be beautiful but Tony doesn't take us out much. Tell you the truth, we're kinda bored. Especially now that Tony took off for a few days. He left out food and said he'd be back in a week!"

Lukan said, "Yep. Bored is the word. We dream of doing something interesting, an adventure even! Like the kind of stuff Rolph always talks about!"

Kab turned and started walking toward the embankment. "Follow me if you want adventure! We have a job to do."

Rolph said, "What do you mean?"

Kab said, "I'll explain once we're down in the creek. And first I'll introduce you to my cat friends."

Lukan said, "Cats? Cool! We love cats. Tony used to have a cat named Tuxedo. He only had one eye but he was full of adventure. He disappeared last year; we think a coyote got him."

When the dogs had climbed down the bank to the creek, Kab introduced them to the waiting cats. "Lukan and Rolph, these two are my friends, Abby and Felix; this third cat is a kitten named Guava. Abby and Felix live with Mike and Nora, next door to me. Guava used to live with her mom and brother in that shack across the creek."

Rolph said, "Wow, you three are pretty big cats!"

Guava was a little nervous and stood behind Felix. Abby looked at her and said, "Come on, little one. They won't hurt us. They're going to help us find your brother!"

Lukan said, "Find her brother? What happened to him?"

Felix said, "Mango is his name. He disappeared through a mysterious tool shed in that old shack in the field across this creek. His mom died, and maybe his brother Ginko also died. Guava here might be the only member of the family left besides Mango and Ginko."

When Felix stopped talking, Rolph stepped closer to Abby and Guava and said, "Come on, Guava. We won't hurt you. We love cats. Let's go find your brothers!"

CHAPTER FIVE

The group took off, crossing the creek and climbing up the opposite bank. Then they started walking carefully towards the shack across the field. Felix said to Rolph, "I don't think the hawk will bother us with you huge dogs with us. Guava told me she thinks a hawk got one of her other brothers, maybe both of them."

They approached the entrance to the shack and began walking slowly. Even though it was a full moon outside, it was very dark inside the shack. As soon as they entered the shack, they stopped and waited for Felix to speak. The shack was full of boxes, bales of hay, gardening tools, and a tool shed. Between two stacks of boxes, they saw the emaciated body of Guava's mother.

Everyone stopped for a moment as Guava whimpered a little, went up to her mother and licked her head. She pulled an empty burlap bag over her, as if to protect her. Then she looked back at the others and nodded. Felix looked around, saw the long rope that was tied around the handle of the tool shed. He said, "Here's what I think we should do. Let's stand single file and hold onto the rope with our teeth. When I say "pull" we'll all pull the rope as hard as we can. I hope we can pull the door open." He looked at Rolph and said, "You pick up the rope in your mouth and the other dogs will line up behind you."

The group lined up—Rolph first, then Lukan and Kab. Abby, Felix and Guava stood aside and watched. Felix yelled out the signal: "PULL!" The dogs started pulling together. At first it seemed they weren't making anything happen. But then—the door started opening slowly with a loud creaking noise. The dogs stopped pulling for a moment, took a breath, and then started again. This time, the door suddenly sprang open!

The dogs dropped the rope and Rolph stepped inside the tool shed. The others followed. They all stood still inside. They were stunned. Abby was the first to speak. "This is impossible! The inside of the shed is much larger than the outside. It's like another room that's as big as the shack itself!" Then she pointed to another door at the end of the shed. "I'll bet that's the door that Mango went through, and maybe Ginko too. Let's check it out!"

Abby began walking slowly through the shed with the others following close behind. They were very careful not to move any of the junk for fear of disturbing a snake—or worse. Finally, they stood facing the door at the back of the shed. It was slightly ajar. Rolph stepped into the opening and pushed against the door with his shoulder. It opened slightly. He gave it another push, and another. Gradually the door opened. When it was open wide enough for him to squeeze through, he stepped through the crack and gave the door another shove, opening it all the way. Everyone stepped through the open door.

They were astounded at what they saw. "It's like a different world," said Lukan.

"How come I see daylight there? It was night when we entered the shack!" Kab was getting nervous. "I don't know about this, guys. This makes no sense."

Lukan said, "Come on. Where's your sense of adventure?" He took a step and motioned for the others to follow. Then he stopped and said, "Hey, last one out should prop the door open. We want to be able to return!" Rolph turned and found a boulder that he pushed inside the door. Then he stopped and said, "Hey, everyone, turn around and look at this! The door we just stepped out of is on the side of this hill. The outside of the door is covered with moss or grass or something. It looks like we just stepped out of a tunnel or a cave, not a shack." Everyone stood still and tried to make sense of what they were looking at. Behind them was the hill. There was no sign of a barn or a street or any other sign of a city like the one they had just came out of. Just the door in the side of the little hill.

CHAPTER SIX

When all of them were standing outside and had blocked the door from closing again, the first thing they noticed was the temperature. "The sun is blazing hot!" Kab never liked the heat. Lukan pointed to a group of trees in the distance and said, "Let's get out of the heat. That little forest looks like it would be a good place to cool off and figure out what we're gonna do next. Come on!" He started walking toward the trees and the others followed.

When the group was about halfway to the trees, they saw a shocking sight. A large creature that looked like it was half dog and half cat was growling and threatening a young human boy! The creature had its back to them. The boy was wearing some kind of animal skin around his waist, and he held a long spear in his hand. He was making jabbing motions at the creature to keep it at bay. Next to the creature was a partially eaten wolf. There were four small wolf cubs huddling and whimpering under a bush near the dead wolf. Next to the boy was a dead deer lying on some kind of sled made of tree branches.

The group stopped and stared. Then Rolph began running towards the creature. He growled ferociously and didn't stop running until he was practically on top of the creature. As the creature was turning towards him, Rolph grabbed its throat and gave it a vigorous shake. Suddenly there was a snapping sound and the creature stopped moving.

"I think it's dead," Abby said when Rolph dropped the creature.

"Definitely dead," Kab said. He trotted up to the creature and said "Eww, what a vicious-looking thing!" The creature was almost as big as Rolph, had two huge fangs, one on each side of its jaws, and the pupils of its eyes were vertical, like a snake's. It was covered in shaggy hair. It had long, vicious-looking claws on its feet.

Turning to Rolph, Kab said, "Good job, I think you saved that boy's life." As he said that, Kab turned to look at the boy. There was an astonished look on the boy's face. Without thinking, Kab spoke to him, "Hey, you're safe now. Are you hurt? My name's Kab." Then he was stunned to hear himself *talking to him!*

The boy also looked stunned to hear a dog talking to him. Then he looked at the rest of the group and said, "Three huge dogs and three huge cats, talking together!" Then he answered Kab, "Yes, I'm okay. But I probably wouldn't have been okay a few minutes later." Turning to Rolph, he said, "You saved my life!"

Rolph was just as shocked as Kab when Kab spoke to the boy. Then Rolph *did the same thing!* He spoke to the boy. "My name's Rolph." Pointing to Lukan he said, "This is Lukan. He's actually a wolf. What was that thing that attacked you? I've never seen anything like it."

Abby, Felix, Guava and Lukan all spoke at the same time. "Yeah, what was that? It was some kind of monster!" Then they, like Rolph, Lukan and Kab, felt a huge shock of surprise to hear themselves speaking to the boy.

The boy put aside his shock at hearing the dogs and cats speaking to him and said, "We call it a `shunka warakin.' Up until recently they didn't come around here very often. They mostly attack deer and boar. It was just my bad luck to be in his hunting territory, I guess." Turning to the dead wolf and the whimpering wolf cubs, he said, "It looks like the creature had just killed the wolf. Those poor cubs, without a mother!" The boy looked at Abby, Felix and Guava and said, "I have NEVER seen cats and dogs together! And I've never heard them talking. Well, *almost* never. Are you friends?"

Felix walked up to him and said, "Yes, we're friends. I rescued this young cat here a few days ago. Guava is her name. Our dog friends, Rolph and Kab, and our wolf friend, Lukan, joined Abby, Guava and me to try to find Guava's brothers." He paused for a moment and then added, "I think we're just as surprised as you are that we can all understand one another." He paused again and said, "Wait a minute. You said `almost' never. What do you mean? Have you heard other dogs and cats talking?"

The boy seemed astonished, but at the same time relieved. "Yes, two cats and a dog. But, if you don't mind, let's all get out of the sun first. There's a spring of cool water in that group of trees over there. I'll tell you about the cats and the dog I met a few days ago who can talk. Maybe you'll be able to meet them."

They all agreed with his suggestion. The boy picked up a long piece of braided leather, both ends of which had been tied around the dead deer's neck and formed a loop. The boy stepped into the loop and held it with his hands at the height of his shoulders. Turning to the cats and dogs he said, "I'm ready. I'll drag this deer and you follow me. And you, Lukan, should go over to the cubs and calm them down, talk to them and tell them to come with us. I'll ask my people to take care of them."

Rolph and Lukan went over to the bushes where the cubs were huddled. Lukan started licking and grooming them, which calmed them down a lot. Then he and Rolph turned and began slowly walking out of the bushes. The cubs looked tentative, but decided to follow them. Then Rolph, Lukan, Kab, the wolf cubs and the cats joined the boy as he started walking to the trees. They fanned out in a tight semicircle as they walked alongside the boy.

Once they entered the shade of the trees, they could hear the sound of water and made a bee line for it. They saw a small stream coming out of the hillside. The stream poured into a little pool of water surrounded by rocks that looked like someone had arranged them into a circle. They all stopped walking. The four wolf cubs stayed close to Rolph and Lukan. Kab said, "Wow, who made this little pool?"

The boy put down the rope and said, "My father and uncle made it. We live at the other end of this group of trees."

There was a moment of silence before anyone could think of what to say. Then Guava said, "You mean there's a town over there?"

The boy said, "What do you mean `town'? There's just a group of huts our families put up before I was born."

Rolph said, "Where we live, people usually live in towns. You know, groups of homes, shops and businesses." Rolph was sitting on his haunches and scratching his ear as he spoke. "If you go back through that door in the hillside we just came out of, you'll see what we're talking about—a town with houses on both sides of the street and grocery stores and drug stores not far away." As he said that, he looked over at the brush-covered door that they had just come through and began to wonder how there could be a town on the other side of the door. *I don't understand how it could be. The door is on the side of that hill. Where are we? And how is it possible that we can speak to the boy?*

The boy sat down at the edge of the pool and scooped some water up to his face and drank deeply before answering. "I've never heard of anything like that. Our people don't live in towns. They live in small groups of huts. But I don't know much about the lands far from here. Maybe there are towns, but I don't think so. Nobody ever talks about towns."

Then he said, "My name's Dakko. I live with my family and three other families at the other end of this little forest. I came out here to hunt for food, like pigs or deer. I hadn't been out here for long before I killed this deer. That was when the shunka warakin started threatening me. I think he must have wanted my deer, although he could have been interested in me. He had just killed the wolf I guess."

Felix said, "Why don't you take us to your family and introduce us? I think we would like to meet them and learn more about this place. It's so different from where we came from." Then he added, "But first, tell us about the other cats and the dog, the ones who you said could talk. As a matter of fact, we're looking for two cats--the brothers of Guava here. Mango and Ginko are their names. They came out here through that same cave we just came out of."

Dakko nodded and said, "Okay. The cat I'm talking about, like I said, was talking to us. He said he was looking for someone, another cat. He said a hawk killed his mother and one of his brothers. He said he thought the other brother might have come out of the same cave he did. Except he didn't call it a cave. He called it . . . what was it? It was a strange name... `closet' I think he called it."

"Yes! Closet! It was a closet in a broken-down barn near

where we live." Kab was getting excited. Then he turned to Guava and said, "You should tell Dakko more about what happened to your family."

Guava sat down and was silent for a moment before answering. "My mom raised me and Mango and our other brother, Ginko. A hawk scared off Ginko; maybe it got him, too. Or maybe Ginko went into the closet to hide. I don't really remember. That's when Mango said he was gonna go through the closet and look for him."

When Guava finished, everyone was quiet for a few moments. Then Dakko said, "Why don't we continue on. We have to go through this little forest for a while and we'll be there. I'm sure my people will be very happy about this deer I'm bringing back. And they will be very interested in hearing your story and especially interested in meeting all you cats, and Rolph, Lukan and Kab." He paused and added, "And I think they'll be happy to welcome these little wolf cubs to our village. I have an idea that we might find them useful! Maybe we can train them to guard our village, especially with Lukan's help!"

The group got up. Dakko picked up the rope again and began dragging the deer through the trees. The rest of the group followed. After a while, the trees thinned. The group stopped when they saw five basket-shaped structures in the distance arranged in a circle. They were made out of small trees woven together, open at the top. Lukan said, "Dakko, maybe you should go ahead of us. Tell everyone about us.

Ask a couple of folks to come out and meet us. What do you think?"

"That's a good idea. Otherwise, the shock might upset everyone." Dakko resumed walking, dragging the deer behind him. The rest of the group waited nervously. Lukan and the others watched as Dakko dropped the deer near a large fire pit and spoke to several children. Then Dakko entered the circle of the huts.

Felix said, "I don't know how I feel right now. Nervous, for sure. But also excited and optimistic. Dakko seems like a great kid. If the others are like him, it will be interesting."

It seemed like a long time before the group could see Dakko emerge from the circle of huts. A woman was walking with him. As they drew near, they came to a stop. Then Dakko motioned for the dogs and cats to come forward. They walked side by side—Felix, Kab, Guava, Lukan, Abby, Rolph and the four wolf cubs. They stopped when they reached Dakko. He turned to the woman next to him and said, "Myra, these are my friends." He introduced them one by one and then added, "Rolph is the one who killed the shunka warakin and probably saved my life and these cubs' lives." Turning to the group he said, "This is my father's sister, Myra."

Myra stepped forward, smiled and said to Rolph, "I can't thank you enough for saving Dakko's life." Turning to the others she said, "And all of you are welcome to our village, meet everyone, and join us for a meal." Then she paused, looked at the cubs, and smiled. "I think these wolf cubs will be very welcome as well." Turning back to Rolph she said, "Not only welcome but useful."

CHAPTER SEVEN

With Myra and Dakko leading, the group walked into a large circular clearing at least 100 yards in diameter. Eight huts were arranged in a large circle around the clearing. In front of each hut was a small enclosure with an animal or two—some kind of fowl in a small cage, and several pig-like animals in a pen of their own. In the middle of the clearing was a partially completed open-air structure made of young trees lashed together and covered by leafy branches. In front of the structure was a fire pit. Several long, low tables and benches made of split logs were arranged inside the structure. It looked like it was some sort of dining area. The ground had been cleared of grass and replaced with fine dirt. Another structure stood some distance away at the edge of the forest. Inside were a dozen or more simple chairs made of logs. A wide, fast-flowing river was visible beyond the edge of the forest.

There were eight adults and four children standing in the clearing. Myra said, "It looks like some of our people are waiting for us."

They stopped and Dakko spoke to the assembled group. "Family and friends, these are the dogs and cats I told you about—the *talking* dogs and cats. Rolph, Lukan and Kab are the dogs. Actually, Lukan is a wolf. The cats are Felix, Guava and Abby. And Rolph not only saved my life by killing the shunka warakin, he rescued these little wolf cubs. The shunka warakin had killed their mother and was threatening me."

Pointing to the open-air structure in the middle of the clearing Myra said, "This is our common dining room. Soon we will make a roof for it but for now we assemble outside. We hope to have our roof completed before the rains come. The other structure is our community hall. Come, let us take a seat in the dining room. Two of our members are preparing a meal for us."

The guests seated themselves on the ground. In deference to their guests, the hosts sat on the ground next to them. Lukan motioned to the wolf cubs to sit next to him. Their curiosity overcame their nervousness, and they got comfortable next to Lukan. Soon another young boy brought over a wide plank and set it on the ground in front of the guests. Then two other people brought out platters of cooked meat and some kind of vegetable. "Looks like cobs of corn," Kab said. The two people introduced themselves as Kassa and Rowalla. Kassa looked like an adolescent boy, and Rowalla looked like she could be his twin sister. They set down the platters on the plank and motioned for the others in the village to come forward. Then Rowalla motioned for everyone to help themselves to the food.

Lukan picked up some bones that still had pieces of meat and gristle attached and dropped them in front of the wolf cubs. As everyone ate, Kab noticed that the dead deer had been set down in front of one of the huts a few yards away from the fire pit. Rowalla said to Kab, "After this meal, we will skin and clean the deer. Then we will salt the meat to preserve it."

Kassa had seated himself next to the four wolf cubs so he could attempt to talk to them. One of the cubs had finished gnawing on his bone and was looking at Kassa with curiosity. Kassa smiled and said, "Do you and your siblings have names?"

The little wolf's eyes grew wide. He whined a little but didn't talk. Lukan watched, and then said, "I talked to them before but in wolf language. They can't talk the way you talk. I think I know why. The wolves didn't come here through the shack like we did. There must have been something about passing through the shack that enabled us to talk to people."

Dakko said, "You mentioned that shack before. You said you came out of a shack and into our land. You remember me telling you before that a cat came here the same way? That cat could talk too. She called herself

Mango. And a very large dog also came here the same way, but much earlier. She told us her name was Keef"

Guava looked startled when she heard Dakko. She said, "Wow! Mango's my sister. Where's Mango now?"

Myra said, "Mango and Keef left a week ago to see if they could find another cat, Mango's brother that she used to live with before she came here. She said the cat's name was Ginko."

Guava got excited and said, "Yes, Mango and Ginko are my sister and brother. I know Mango used to go into the closet in the shack, and I think Ginko did also."

Myra said, "Could you show us the shack after we finish eating?"

CHAPTER EIGHT

During the meal, Rolph said to Myra, "You said you thought the wolf cubs might be useful to you. How so?"

Myra thought for a few moments before answering. "Well, that creature that you killed, the shunka warakin, was not the only one around here. We have encountered them before. Not long ago three of them raided our livestock and made off with several animals. Although their hunting territory is across the river, several of them have crossed the river and attacked our livestock. We were thinking we could try to befriend one of the wolfpacks that live some distance away and get them to move closer to our village. That way they could warn us when the shunka warakin approached, and perhaps even attack them. But it would probably require more than one wolf; very likely it would take two or three attacking together to kill one of those creatures."

Rolph said, "Maybe one of us could train these little wolves to approach the nearby wolves to see if any of them could work with us. To guard the community, or even attack the creatures. Lukan, being a wolf himself, would be the logical one to work with the little wolves; maybe even take them out and introduce them to the nearby wolves."

Lukan was following the conversation closely as he watched the little cubs eating. "I think I could train these little guys as guards. They're still pretty young, maybe too young to actually approach the local wolves. But I would like to give it a try. Being a grown wolf myself, I might be able to convince the wolves around here to join with us in hunting down some of the shunka warakin. I mean, working with Rolph, of course. That shunka warakin wasn't the first creature that Rolph has killed. He used to chase down and kill hyenas in Africa."

Myra looked puzzled. "What are hyenas? Are they like the shunka warakin?"

Rolph said, "Not really. They're really vicious creatures that look like dogs but are supposedly distantly related to cats; at least that's what people in Africa said. They hunt other animals in packs. The farmers in Africa used to train large dogs like us to hunt them down."

Myra said, "You mention a place called Africa. We have never heard of such a place. We haven't heard of cities and towns, either. Maybe you can tell us more later, but first we have more important matters to talk about."

Dakko noticed that everyone seemed to be finished with

their meal. "Let's go relax inside our community hall." He gestured to the community hall. "Some of the elders will tell you a little more about what Mango and Keef had planned to do."

Dakko and Myra led the group to the community hall. Lukan found a grassy spot and told the wolf cubs to get comfortable. Rowalla and her brother Kassa sat next to the cubs. Myra smiled as the others did the same. In a few minutes other members of the community began coming in to the hall. Soon it seemed like the hall was filled with over a dozen people in addition to Dakko and Myra.

An older man spoke, "Welcome to our little community. It has been over a week since we met others like yourselves who could talk to us, a large cat and a large dog. Mango and Keef are their names. When they learned of the danger that we face from the menacing behavior of the shunka warakin, they came up with a plan."

Lukan said, "I would love to hear about your plan, and to help out if we can. Maybe, until Mango and Keef return, we could get started. As I said, I'd like to see if I could interest the wolves in this area to join together to hunt down and chase off the shunka warakin. What exactly were Mango and Keef planning, do you know?"

Dakko said, "Keef described it as something like what you were thinking. She would try to talk a pack of wolves into helping us hunt down the shunka warakin."

Rolph said, "Well, I think any wolves in the area might be a little skeptical of a plan that a cat and dog might come up with."

Kab sighed and said to Rolph, "Let's don't be too critical, my friend. I, for one, think we should hear Dakko's plan."

Dakko smiled and said, "Thanks, Kab." Turning to Rolph and Lukan, he said, "You're right that wolves might not take seriously a plan proposed by a cat and a dog, even a large cat like Mango and a HUGE dog like Keef. After all, they're not known to be fighters, especially against a large vicious monster like the shunka warakin. But I think the idea was to invite several of the wolves here to meet us, the people, and talk about a strategy."

Lukan said, "Hey, now that Kab, Rolph and I are here with the other Maine Coon cats -- Felix, Abby and Guava -- I think the wolves might take us seriously. Especially since Rolph killed the shunka warakin and rescued these wolf cubs."

CHAPTER NINE

There was silence for a few minutes as everyone thought about what had been said. Then, to everyone's surprise and delight, Mango, Ginko and Keef emerged from the trees surrounding the little settlement. And even more surprising was who was with them—two wolves! One appeared to be a mature female and the other looked like a juvenile male. They walked proudly, but respectfully, as they entered the clearing alongside the two cats and Keef. As they approached the center of the hall, they stopped in amazement at what they saw. Then Keef spoke: "Friends, and guests. I think I am just as full of wonder as you are. Cats, dogs, and even young wolves!"

Mango turned to Ginko and spoke, "I see our sister, Guava! And two other cats and three dogs I recognize from where I come from!" Mango and Ginko walked forward and rubbed against Guava. They smiled at Felix,

Abby, Kab, Rolph and Lukan. Then Mango stopped, turned to Keef and said, "Keef, my dear friend, these cats and dogs are from our neighborhood, where we used to live before we came here. The dogs are Kab and Rolph, and the wolf is Lukan. The cats are Felix, Abby and our dear sister Guava. But the four other wolves—where did they come from and how did they get here?"

Then, Keef turned to the wolves that had accompanied her and Ginko and Mango, and said the same thing to them in their own language. Lukan and the rescued wolf cubs looked shocked when Keef did that.

Kab and the others seemed to be stunned into silence. But then Lukan spoke. "I suppose we should explain how all this came to be—how we came to be here, and how these young wolf cubs came under our protection." Turning to Felix he said, "I think our good cat friend, Felix, should do the honors since he's the one who got everything started."

Felix stood and said, "It all came about quite by accident. I was exploring an old shack near where I live and came upon this young kitten Guava here and took her back to my home. She told me she had a brother named Mango and a sister named Ginko. She said those two had disappeared. I introduced her to Abby, and we decided to help Guava look for her brother and sister. We asked these two wonderful dogs here, Kab and Rolph, and their friend the wolf Lukan, to help us."

At that point, Dakko said to Mango and Keef, "Rolph

here is the one who saved me from the shunka warakin." Then, turning to the group, Dakko said, "Maybe Mango and Keef should introduce the two wolves they've brought here."

Keef spoke to the elder wolf and translated her reply for the group. "This is Umukaha, and her son is Ukaha. They have told their pack of our request to put a stop to the attacks by the shunka warakin tribe, and the pack has agreed to help us come up with a plan." Then, Keef continued, "Let's ask these four wolf cubs to tell us about themselves."

Lukan turned to the four cubs and spoke to them in their language. "Introduce yourselves and tell us what you know about the shunka warakin, where they live and hunt, how many there are, if you know."

The oldest cub said, "I am Seema." Pointing to the other cubs, she said, "These are my little brothers. Our mother hadn't given them names yet because they are still young. I am my mother's oldest daughter now that my sister has left our pack and joined another pack. As Dakko can confirm, our mother was killed by the shunka warakin." Seema looked at Umukaha and Ukaha, then continued, "I think I know where there is a group of shunka warakin nearby."

Lukan repeated what Seema had said to Dakko and the other people. Then he asked Seema, "How many and how near?"

Myra said, "I can answer that. There are only a few, maybe only four or five. We saw them cross the river a few days ago, kill some of our animals, and return across the river."

Lukan looked surprised. "How could anyone cross that river? It's very swift and wide."

Rolph turned to Myra and said, "In the distance I can see what looks like a huge uprooted tree lying across the river. Is that how the shunka warakin came across, using the tree as a bridge?"

"Myra said, "Yes. The tree isn't very wide, and the force of the river causes the tree to wobble a bit. Even so, some of the shunka warakin have been able to crawl across."

Kab spoke up. "I Have an idea. Let's go over to the river bank and take a look at where this end of the tree rests on the bank. Maybe we can dislodge the tree."

Almost everyone in the little community seemed to be curious to find out what Kab had in mind and followed him to the river.

CHAPTER TEN

It didn't take more than a few minutes to reach the river bank. From there, the group turned left and followed the bank another few minutes to the spot where the top of the tree was lying on the bank. "Wow! That's a huge tree—lots of branches," Rolph said.

"And it looks like most of the branches are firmly buried in the mud," Lukan said.

Umukaha turned to Lukan and said, "I have an idea. My pack had agreed to help put a stop to the attacks by the shunka warakin. I can return to my pack and tell them about this fallen tree. Maybe they can come here, and together maybe we'll be able to dislodge the trunk from the riverbank so the tree can float down the river."

Lukan said, "That's a good idea. I hope there will be enough of us to do that."

Umukaha said to Lukan, "Why don't you and the others

come back with me and Ukaha to our pack. Maybe that will convince them that we mean business!"

Lukan and Keef nodded. Then Keef added, "It would be a good idea for Rolph, Kab and the cats to come with us and meet your pack. I think the pack might be impressed if they see what kind of group we are. And we could tell them the nearby community of people want to work with the pack."

Umukaha nodded and said, "I like that plan." She turned to Kab, Rolph and the cats and asked, "What do you think? Are you up for a little adventure?"

Kab said, "Sure, as long as it's not too much adventure." The cats nodded.

Myra said, "Dakko and I will wait here by the tree. We'll try to come up with an idea for dislodging the tree from the bank."

Umukaha said, "Okay! Let's get going."

Umukaha and Ukaha started walking and the others followed. Felix, Abby and Guava were a little nervous about the idea of meeting a pack of wolves, even though they were already acquainted with Lukan, Kab and Rolph. And they were encouraged that Mango, Ginko and Keef would introduce them to the wolf pack.

The sun was no longer overhead an hour later when the group approached the area where Umukaha said her pack lived. She turned and said, "Keef, Ukaha and I will go on ahead and meet with our pack's leader. We'll bring Seema and her three siblings with us and tell them about the group and our hope to come up with a plan."

Lukan said, "Do you think Rolph and I should go with you? I'm a wolf and Rolph is a huge wolf-like dog."

Umukaha said, "Maybe you two, Kab and the cats should wait until Keef tells the pack about you." Lukan nodded. Umukaha, Ukaha, Seema and the cubs continued on to where the pack lived. The rest of the group watched.

In a few minutes Umukaha saw four wolves waiting for them. She, Keef and Ukaha walked ahead and greeted the four wolves. Then she turned and motioned for Seema and the other cubs to approach. Seema told the other cubs not to be nervous, and together they rejoined Umukaha and Ukaha.

Umukaha introduced the four wolves who had greeted them. "These four are Waka, the oldest female of our pack, Gaytu, the oldest male, their daughter Weema, and their son Keemu. Waka has invited all of you to come into the compound and talk about the fallen tree. They want to meet the other cats besides Mango, too."

Keef nodded, turned and walked back to invite Lukan, Rolph, Kab and the cats to join them. Everyone followed Keef back to the compound.

CHAPTER ELEVEN

The wolf compound was impressive. It was a flat, grassy area surrounded by trees and bushes. The wolves had put together individual family shelters for themselves made from tree branches, grass, small rocks and large stones. Beyond the compound was a vast grassland interspersed with bushes and small trees, the perfect habitat for rabbits and deer.

Waka turned to Keef and said something. Keef translated her reply. "She wants to meet with the people I told her about, and take a look at the tree that fell across the river. She says the wolves also have been plagued by the shunka warakin. She is fond of Mango and Ginko, who had told her about the people and their community."

Lukan looked at the others and asked if anyone would object to leading Waka and other wolves to the people's compound. Everyone agreed.

Waka and four other wolves joined the dogs and cats in

an hour-long walk back to where Myra, Dakko and four other people were standing near the tree. The wolves all walked around the end of the tree that was buried in the mud. Gaytu said, "This tree looks firmly stuck in the mud. But I think with a lot of us working hard we can dig out most of the mud around the trunk. But first we'll have to break off most of the branches just to be able to get to the trunk itself."

Dakko said, "Well, let's get to it! My aunt and I brought some axes, and we can chop off enough branches to get access to the trunk."

Dakko and Myra started chopping the larger branches. The other people started breaking off the smaller branches. In less than an hour most of the branches were cut or broken off the trunk. Then the wolves and dogs started digging on both sides of the trunk until the buried part of the trunk was exposed. Myra, Dakko and the other four people began wedging some of the larger cut branches under the trunk until six branches were firmly underneath.

Dakko said, "Okay, one person should stand at each branch and press down on my signal. At the same time all the wolves and dogs should start pushing this end of the tree to the left toward the river. You cats should keep digging under the tree to help free it from the mud."

Everyone took their places and waited for Dakko to give the signal. Once everyone was in place, Dakko yelled out, "NOW !!" As soon as he and the other people started shoving down on the branches, the tree began to rise off the mud. At that point, the wolves and dogs started pushing on the tree. As they did so, the cats began digging furiously at the dirt and mud underneath in order to allow the tree to move more freely.

The trunk of tree began sliding to the left. The bottom of the tree that had been resting on the other bank started moving slowly to the right. Soon, the group's efforts moved the trunk very close to the bank of the river. The top of the tree was now almost at the edge of the river. Dakko yelled, "Okay! One last shove! Give it all your strength. Go!"

Eveyone pushed together and the trunk slid across the bank and into the water. Lukan, Kab, Keef and Rolph followed it in and pushed against it to get it fully into the stream. On the other bank, the top of the tree was sliding into the water. Then they stopped, and everyone looked in amazement as the entire tree was caught in the force of the current and started floating downstream.

Dakko and Myra yelled out at the same time, "Yesss!" The other people started dancing around and hugging each other. The wolves howled in unison. Lukan, Kab, Keef and Rolph got out of the water, shook themselves, and howled in joy. Felix, Abby, Freddy, Mango, Guava and Ginko stepped a little way into the water, washed themselves off, and joined in the howling with the dogs and wolves.

Everyone stood on the bank and watched as the tree disappeared down the river.

CHAPTER TWELVE

Myra turned to Lukan and said, "This has been a wonderful day. We can't thank you enough. Those beasts, the shunka warakin, will not be able to come across the river and attack us any longer." The other people hugged each other and looked thankfully at all their new friends.

Kab said, "I think we should be getting back to our homes. The people we live with will probably be wondering where we are."

Dakko said, "We can walk with you back to the hillside where you said you had propped open a door."

Kab, Lukan, Rolph, Keef, Felix, Abby, Freddy, Guava, Mango and Ginko stood together and looked at the people and the wolves. Felix said, "Okay, let's get going before it gets dark."

The group walked slowly back. Soon, they could see the hillside. When they got there, they could see the boulder propping open the door in the hillside. Rolph turned and said to the others, "I am sure going to miss you Dakko and Myra, and for sure all you wolves. It's not going to be the same going back to our boring old town."

Keef looked at Rolph, the wolves and everyone else. Then she sighed and said, "I think I've become very attached to this place and all the people and wolves. I hope it won't break anyone's heart, but I think I'll stick around for awhile. I don't really have a home in where I came from. The people I lived with moved away and didn't take me with them. So, this place has become my real home. But I know how to return if I want to. And for sure you all know how to come back through the shack for a visit, any time you want!"

Nobody spoke for a moment. Then Lukan said, "Keef, I'm sure we're all gonna miss you. And I sure hope you decide to come back through the shack. I'm pretty sure I could talk Tony into inviting you to live with us." Kab, Rolph and the cats looked sad, but at the same time agreed that Keef would be welcomed at Tony's house.

The group then walked over to the boulder and Rolph said, "All right, I'm gonna move this boulder and hold open the doorway into the hillside. Everyone should walk through and I'll follow." He rolled the boulder away from the doorway and held the door open. One by one the cats and dogs walked through the doorway. Rolph was the last. He stopped in the doorway, turned and said to Keef, the wolves and the people, "Okay, Keef and everyone. You know where we live and how to get there." Turning to Dakko, he said, "If you'd like to pay us a visit, I think you'll be shocked when you see how different our town is. But if you decide to check it out, here's what you need to do. When you come through the tunnel you'll be inside a shack. Wait until dark so you won't be too shocked by how different it is. Then leave the shack, turn right, cross the field, and you'll come to Tony's house on the right side of the street. Just yell out my name and I'll meet you at the gate."

Dakko shook his head and said, "Thanks, but I don't think I want to do that. This is my world. I'm not part of Tony's world. Besides, how would I even talk to him? You all can speak to me, and we can understand each other. What kind of language does Tony speak?" He paused and said, "But thanks for the invitation."

With that, Dakko and Myra rubbed Rolph and kissed his head. Then Rolph stood up on his hind legs, wrapped his front paws around Dakko's neck and licked him. Dakko said, "Thanks for saving my life, Rolph. I'll never forget that."

Rolph stood back down and took a few steps further into the doorway. He rolled the stone back to cover the doorway and was gone.

ABOUT THE AUTHOR

I graduated from San Francisco State University in 1972 with a B.A. in Creative Writing.

I served in Peace Corps from 1972 to 1974 (Ethiopia and Eritrea). In 2000 my memoir, "Asmara, A Memoir", was included in the *Peace Corps Writers* anthology, "Eritrea Remembered: Recollections and Photos by Peace Corps Volunteers." I self-published a collection of aerogrammes, memoirs and photos from my two years there—***Life as a Peace Corps Volunteer, Ethiopia and Eritrea, 1972-74.***

I earned a Master's Degree in International Communication in 1976, a Master's Degree in Librarianship in 1977, and a J.D. from Golden Gate University in 1991. Before law school I worked as a school librarian for nine years.

While a law student, I served on the Law Review and published an article, "Qualified Immunity for INS Church-Busters? Presbyterian Church (U.S.A.) v. United States." *Ninth Circuit Survey*, Volume 20, Number 1, Spring 1990.

I practiced criminal law for 23 years (1988-2011) in the California Attorney General's Office in San Francisco. During that time, in addition to arguing criminal cases in the California courts, I taught for 13 semesters in Golden

Gate University's "Appellate Advocacy" program part time as an Adjunct Professor.

I retired as a prosecutor in 2011 and volunteered for four years representing military veterans seeking to increase their retirement benefits. During that time, I began writing fiction and memoirs, all of which are available on https://www.amazon.com.

My first novel was *Stolen Identity*, published in 2015 by Andrew Benzie Books. Also published by Andrew Benzie Books were: *Stolen Identity*'s sequel, *Unfinished Business*, (2017); *A Time Away from Time* (2023); *The Starlight Commune* (2024); *A Voyage through the Interstice* (2024); *Tales of Nicolas Flamel, Time Traveler* (2024); and *The Happy Wanderer* (2024). You can find my books on https://www.amazon.com by typing in my name and a title. You can also find my self-published novels, stories and memoirs there.

In 2021 I self-published the novel *The Mystic and the Warrior* (an embittered Persian émigré joins forces with a disgruntled Turkish army officer in an attempt to overthrow the Turkish government) and the novel *Trial and Error* (the third one in the trilogy that began with *Stolen Identity*).

Also in 2021 I self-published a collection of short stories: *Collected Stories*. One of the stories in that collection, "One More Race Before We Die," was published earlier in 2019 in the University of Hawaii online magazine *Vice-Versa*. The other stories in that collection were "My Brother's Keeper" (loosely based on my younger brother's murder), "Gino di Lampedusa" (the story of a rogue genie in Las Vegas), and "Whitethorn, 1969" (the story of a group of back-to-the-land hippies confronted by a rogue group of anarchists who are terrorizing the local town).

www.ingramcontent.com/pod-product-compliance
Lightning Source LLC
Chambersburg PA
CBHW071225170626
46809CB00005BA/1932